Sparky and Dino the Colourful Snails

Catherine Beach

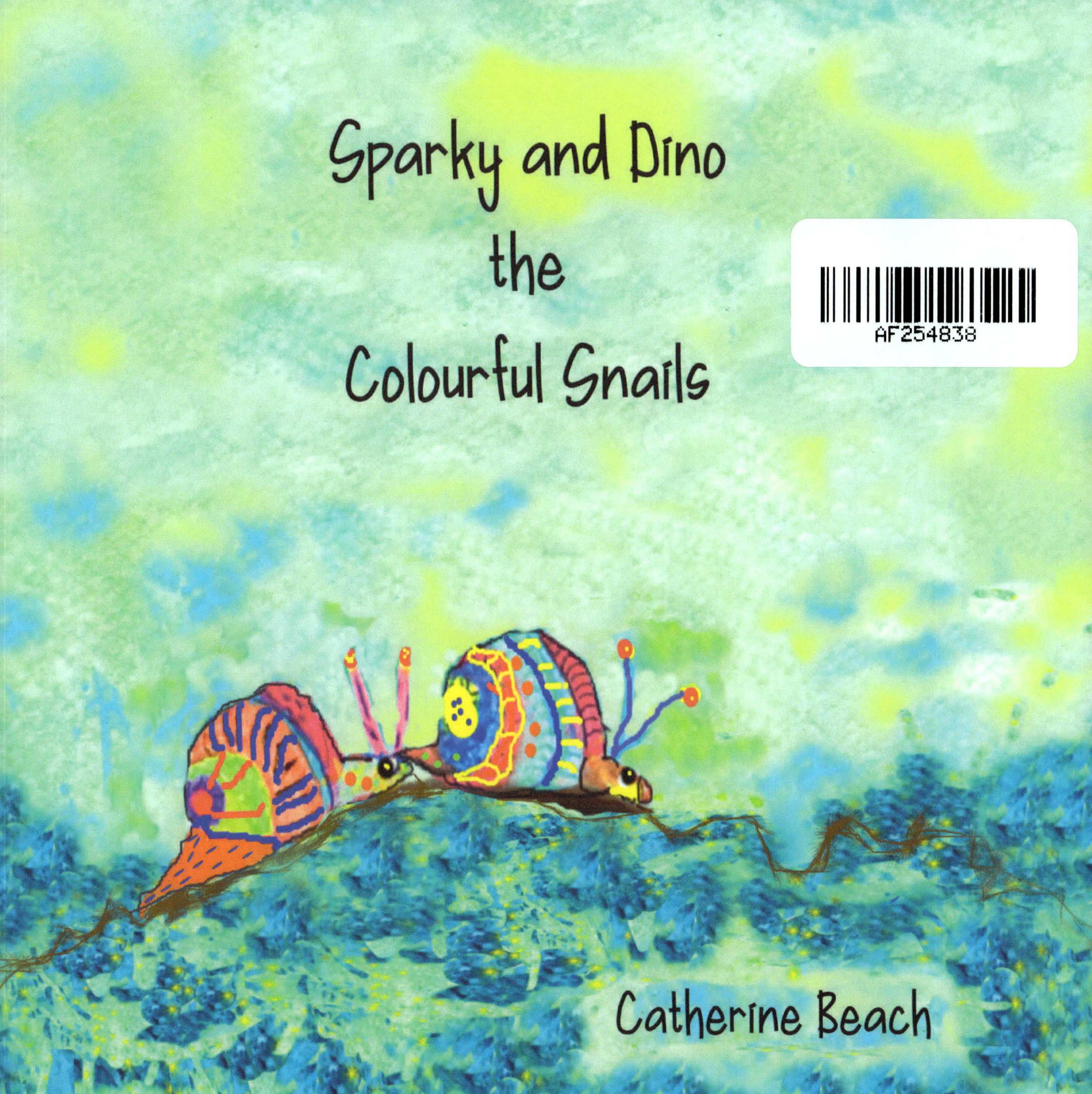

Hello
meet
Sparky and Dino

Sparky and Dino are two little snails,
with stripes on their backs and very long tails.

Their home is a rock with a hole in the side,
where they are safe and can quickly hide.

They often explore all through the night,
using their eyes as great big lights.

They slide along, leaving silvery trails that sparkle in the moonlight like shimmering scales.

They see lots of creatures
that live in the sea,
and often wonder
how that would be.

Sparky and Dino want to learn to sail,
to travel the world and meet other snails.

Sparky and Dino went out one day,
down to the wharf to look at the bay.

They watched the boats all bobbing about,
when they noticed a creature with a very long snout.

Another day for Sparky and Dino;
they headed to the wharf for their cappuccino.

With eyes wide open, they looked around,
and caught a glimpse of something brown.

They slid down a post to the water's edge,
where they saw a turtle resting near a ledge.

The snails are curious, so they listened in,
they knew a story was about to begin.

The turtle looked up bursting with glee,
then rested her head to look at the sea.

Sparky and Dino tapped on her shell,
and she said, 'Hello there, my name is Narelle.'

When the turtle turned around, she saw the snails, and gave them a wink, 'Let's go for a sail!'

'Hang on tight and, come swim with me...
to a special place where more snails will be.'

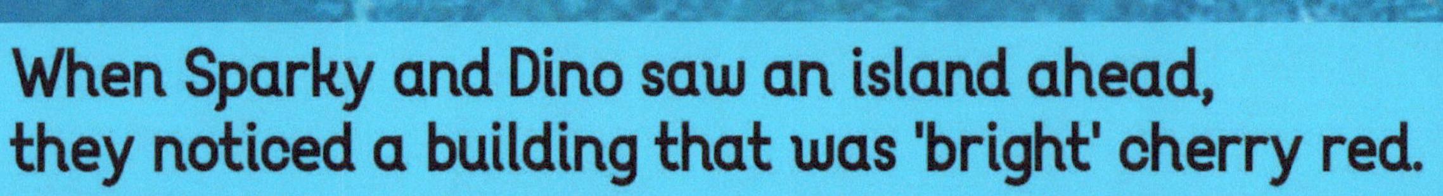

When Sparky and Dino saw an island ahead,
they noticed a building that was 'bright' cherry red.

Their eyes took in many colours to see;
they wondered if this was where more snails would be!

The snails played soccer on the golden sand,
all dressed up like a music band.

They laugh, they dance and tell lots of tales,
and live happily ever after as the 'Cuban Snails.'

Did you know!
Cuban snails are
the most colourful
snails in the world!

Good Night   Sleep Tight

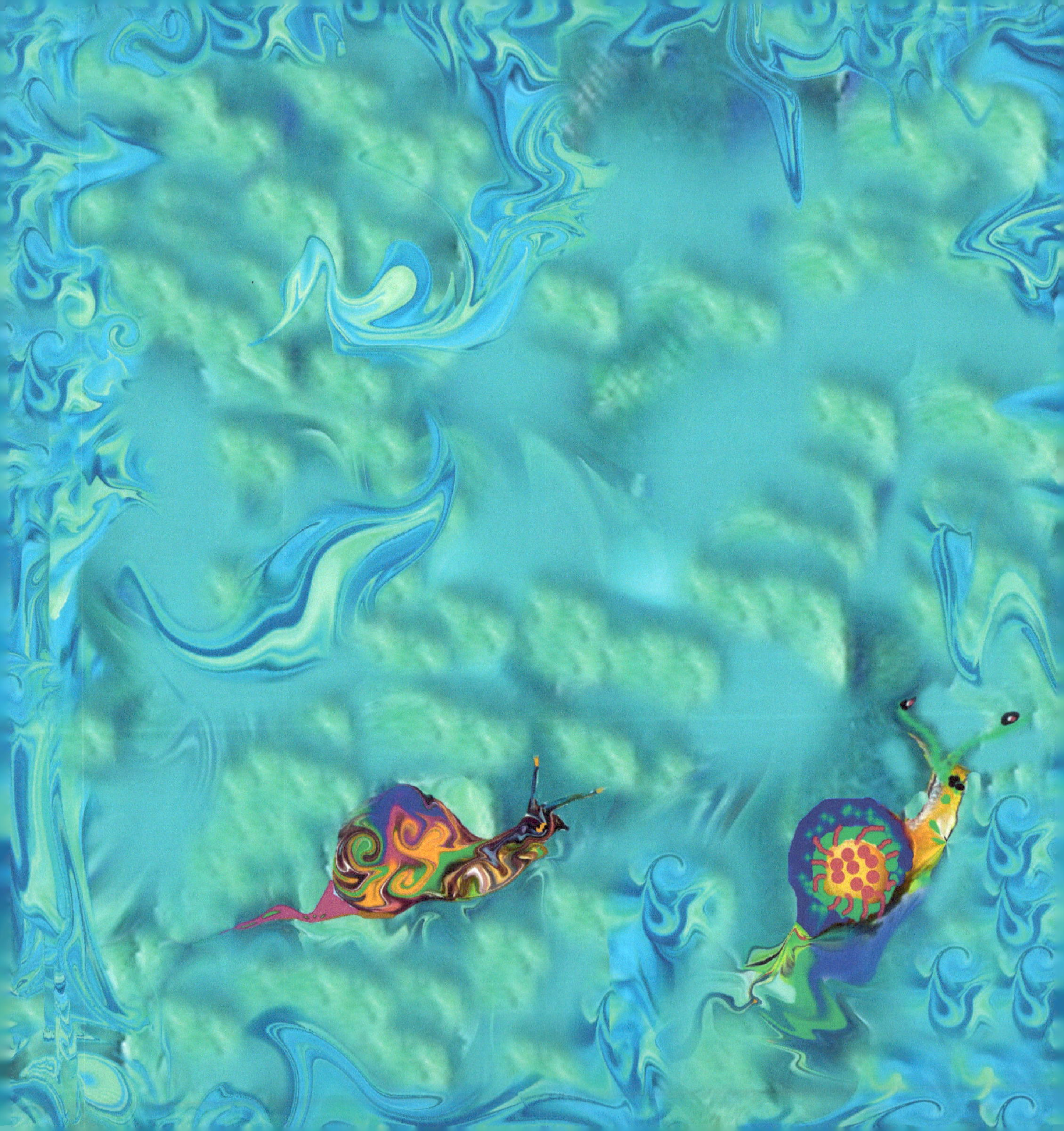

A story to be told

Beads of Paradise welcomes Books for Little Bandits
Catherine Beach is an author and illustrator of Books for Little Bandits

It all started when Catherine moved her city life to the country…all in the name of love. Living on a mixed cropping and sheep farm, surrounded by vast open space and never-ending plains with lively wildlife, Catherine found the pace to be much slower and began to miss the hustle and bustle of city life. This was when she decided to bring her own hustle and bustle to the farm by fulfilling her creative passion.

It started with Beads of Paradise because every day on the farm was like a new day in paradise (well…not always!). Beads of Paradise became her haven. Catherine handcrafted costume jewellery and accessories for brides for over a decade. Suddenly, Covid took control, and whilst there were fewer weddings, there were more babies…

This led Catherine to her next escapade; Books for Little Bandits. Catherine had been spending a lot of time painting, using printmaking and digital techniques in her art, and she has been known to tell a good story or two. Books for Little Bandits is a collection of children's storybooks that uses a combination of Catherine's art and storytelling techniques to give families insight into life's adventures in a fun and colourful way.

"All it took was a paintbrush…and an idea and I went for it! (Catherine)

Who knows what the next book could be about!

Books for Little Bandits

A collection of children's books individually handcrafted using printing techniques, painting, and storytelling.

www.booksforlittlebandits.com

Catherine Beach

ISBN 978-0-6455411-1-3

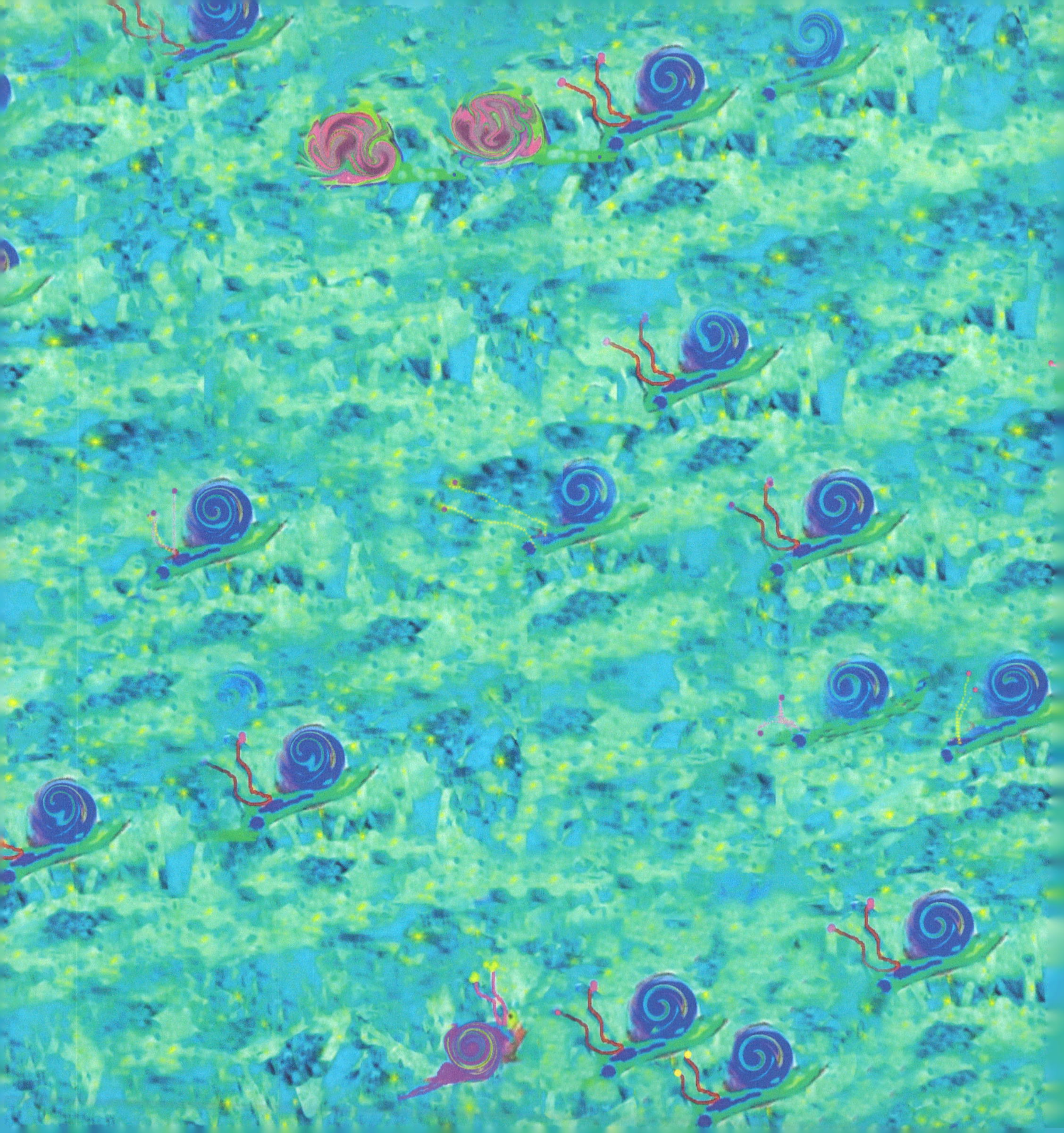